TROLL
TALES

retold by
Corinne Denan
illustrated by
Ed Parker

Troll Associates

Troll Tales: The Grumpy Old Troll, Naden; *Cinderlad and the Trolls,* Grimm.

Copyright © 1980 by Troll Associates, Mahwah, N.J.

Library of Congress# 79-66327
ISBN 0-89375-322-X/0-89375-321-1 (pb)

CONTENTS

The Grumpy Old Troll

The oldest Troll on Troll Mountain was very old. No one really knew how old he was, because Trolls can't count. They could have learned to count if they wanted to, of course. But, according to the way Trolls look at things, there is nothing worth counting. So no one knew how old anyone was on Troll Mountain. But life went on, just the same.

The oldest Troll on Troll Mountain was also very grumpy. But no one knew why.

"Maybe he has an upset stomach," said the Troll's daughter. "He looks a little green to me."

"He *is* green!" exclaimed the Troll's wife.

"I mean a little more green than usual," said the Troll's daughter.

But that wasn't it. The old Troll did not have an upset stomach. He didn't know it, but he had a toothache. He had had a toothache for years and years, and that's why he was so grumpy. But no Troll had ever had a toothache before. So the old Troll did not know he was grumpy because of a bad tooth. He just knew he was grumpy.

When folks are grumpy, they sometimes do

7

strange things. So the old Troll started to steal shoes from the people who lived in the valley. But what was even more strange was that he only stole *left* shoes. He took them out of closets and out of shoe boxes. He took them off doorsteps, and even right off people's feet. And he piled all the shoes in a big clearing up on Troll Mountain. The old Troll didn't look at it as stealing. It just made him feel less grumpy. Sometimes it even gave him a chuckle or two.

The people in the valley were not chuckling. They did not like running around with one shoe on and one shoe off. Everyone was *very* upset.

But no one was more upset than the cobbler. He didn't have any shoes to repair because there was no sense repairing just one shoe. And what was the use of making new shoes? After all, no one wanted to pay for a new pair of shoes if the left shoe was going to be stolen. And they *knew* it was going to be stolen.

The cobbler didn't know what to do. "What am I going to do?" he asked. His wife did not know. "I don't know," she said.

"We must catch the one who is stealing the shoes," said Galen, the cobbler's son. "It must be a Troll. And I'm going to find him."

"How can you do that?" asked the cobbler.

"I'll find a way," said Galen. But he had no idea at all how to find the old Troll. He did not even know what a Troll looked like.

"Just tell me how I will recognize a Troll when I see one," said Galen.

"That's easy," said the cobbler. "A Troll is very small and green. He has a long beard. His head is pointed. His nose is shaped like a turnip, and there is a large wart on the end of it."

So very early the next morning, Galen set off in the direction of Troll Mountain. He carried a sack that his mother had filled with food. He was wearing a new pair of boots his father had made.

It so happened that just as Galen headed up the mountain, the old Troll headed down toward the valley. Lately the Troll had been getting up very early, so he could look for left shoes. There was hardly a left shoe in the entire valley, and this made the old Troll grumpier than ever.

In a small clearing, Galen and the Troll bumped right into each other. The Troll was wearing an old hat pulled way down over his face. His beard was tucked neatly into his shirt. So Galen did not recognize him.

"Good morning, sir," said Galen.

"Humph," said the grumpy old Troll.

10

"Won't you join me for a bite to eat?" asked Galen.

The old Troll saw Galen's shiny new boots. Here was a prize indeed! Perhaps it would be better to talk to this foolish lad for a while until he figured out a way to get that beautiful left boot.

So the old Troll sat down to share Galen's food. But he did not get too close to the young man. He didn't want to take any chances. He knew that if someone touches a Troll on the shoulder, the Troll must be that person's friend forever. There is no way out of it, for that is the way things are with Trolls.

"I am hunting an old Troll who I am sure is stealing all the left shoes in the valley," said Galen pleasantly. "Have you seen him?"

Under his breath, the old Troll said, "Stealing, humph. The very idea of calling it stealing!" Out loud he said, "How would I know him if I saw him?"

"Oh, you would know him right away," answered Galen. "He is small and green with a long beard. His head is pointed. His nose is shaped like a turnip, and there is a large wart on the end of it."

"He must be handsome, indeed," said the old

Troll. And then he couldn't help adding, "In fact, he must look a lot like me."

"Oh, not at all," said Galen. "You don't look anything like that."

"Humph!" said the old Troll. "Then what do I look like?"

Galen thought for a moment. Then he said, "Actually, you look a bit like my grandfather."

The old Troll thought that was about the funniest thing he had ever heard. He began to laugh, despite his grumpiness. He laughed and laughed and laughed. In fact, he laughed so hard that the piece of bread he had been eating became stuck in his throat. Then he began to choke. Galen slapped him on the back. And as he did, his other hand rested on the Troll's shoulder.

The Troll stopped choking, but the damage was done. Now, whether he liked it or not, he was Galen's friend forever.

"You've ruined everything!" cried the Troll. For even though he had to be Galen's friend, there was nothing to prevent him from being grumpy about it.

"You might as well come with me," said the Troll. And off he went up Troll Mountain.

Galen ran after him. High up the mountain,

they came to a large clearing. Galen could not believe his eyes. There, in a huge pile, were hundreds of shoes—*thousands* of shoes. Black shoes and white shoes, red shoes and blue shoes. Shoes with pointy toes and shoes with round toes. Shoes with ties, straps, and buckles. Big shoes and little shoes. Dancing shoes and hunting shoes— and every one was a *left* shoe!

"I don't believe it!" said Galen.

"Humph," said the grumpy old Troll. "There they are. You can take them all back. I just borrowed them, anyway."

"But how can I carry all these shoes?" asked Galen.

"Humph," said the old Troll again. "I suppose I'll have to help you. Drat this friend business!"

The old Troll put two fingers between his pointy teeth and whistled. In a few seconds, the whole mountain was alive with Trolls. Galen had never imagined there were so many Trolls in all the world. They were dancing and jumping and running all around the pile of shoes.

"Let's go," said the grumpy Troll. "Everybody take an armful of shoes and follow me."

The line of little Trolls, with Galen in the front, stretched all the way from Troll Mountain down

14

into the valley. Never had the people in the valley seen such an amazing sight! Galen marched in front, leading the way. Right behind him was the grumpy old Troll. Behind him were all sizes and shapes of Trolls. And every one had an armful of left shoes. It was a day to remember.

The people of the valley were so happy to get all their shoes back that they decided to hold a great celebration. They even invited the Trolls. There were speeches and food and games and a good deal of dancing. Trolls are especially fond of dancing.

By and by, Galen saw the old Troll sitting gloomily under the town fountain. "Why aren't you dancing?" Galen asked.

"Because I don't feel like it, that's why," said the old Troll. "I haven't danced for nearly as long as I can remember—not since I started to get grumpy, years and years ago."

Galen took a closer look at the Troll. "Your face seems rather puffy," he said. "You probably have a bad tooth. Do you have a toothache?"

"What's a toothache?" asked the grumpy old Troll.

"Just open your mouth," said Galen. The Troll opened his mouth, and Galen looked inside.

"Just as I thought. Come with me," said Galen, and he led the old Troll to his father's cobbler shop. "Open your mouth," he said again. Then Galen picked up a pair of pliers, placed them firmly around the bad tooth, and pulled.

"Ouch!" yelled the old Troll. "What are you doing?"

"I'm getting rid of your toothache," said Galen. And he held up the bad tooth.

The old Troll couldn't believe it. For the first time in years and years, he didn't feel grumpy.

"Now let's go back to the celebration," said Galen.

The old Troll just looked at him, and said, "Humph!"

Sometimes, old habits are hard to break.

Cinderlad and the Trolls

A long, long time ago, there were three brothers. The two older brothers said that the youngest was good for nothing but emptying the cinders from the fireplace, and he believed them. He believed everything they said.

One day, all three brothers went to the King's palace to seek their fortunes. The oldest took a job as the coachman's helper. The middle one took a job as the gardener's helper. And the youngest took a job as the King's kitchen helper.

Every day, as the youngest brother took out the cinders, his brothers would make fun of him, and call him "Cinderlad." But Cinderlad did not mind. He always had a smile on his face, which made everyone else in the palace very fond of him. And this made his brothers hate him more than ever.

It so happened that behind the King's palace was a lake, and on the other side of the lake lived an ugly old Troll. This Troll had seven silver ducks that liked nothing better than to swim in the lake. Every time the King looked out across the lake, he saw the silver ducks. And every time he saw them, he wished they were his.

One day, the two older brothers decided to get Cinderlad into trouble. So when the coachman passed by, they began talking to one another.

"Did you hear what Cinderlad said?" asked one.

"No," replied the other. "Tell me."

"He said it would be easy for him to get the seven silver ducks for the King."

Of course, the coachman went straight to the King and told him what he had heard. At once, the King called for Cinderlad to be brought before him.

"I have heard that you can get me the seven silver ducks," said the King.

"Oh dear," sighed Cinderlad. "Who would say such a thing?"

"Your brothers," replied the King. "Your brothers said it would be easy for you to do."

"Then it must be true," said the lad. "I will do it, but first I must have a sack of grain."

So the King gave him the sack of grain, and Cinderlad rowed across the lake. When he reached the opposite shore, he scattered the grain about, and then made a path of grain back to his boat. Then he sat down to wait.

Before long, the seven silver ducks had followed the path of grain, and were all in the boat. So the lad began to row back across the lake. But when he was halfway across, he heard the ugly old Troll stomping and puffing on the shore.

"Who dares to steal my silver ducks?" roared the Troll.

"It is I," called Cinderlad, "the King's kitchen helper."

"Come back here!" roared the Troll.

"Perhaps I shall," replied the lad. "Perhaps I shall." But he kept on rowing until he was back at the King's palace.

When the King saw the silver ducks, he was very pleased. He praised the lad for his cunning and his bravery. But the two brothers only grew more jealous. And they tried to think of some way to make trouble for their younger brother.

It so happened that the ugly old Troll had a magnificent bedspread made of spun silver and gold. The King wanted nothing more than to own it himself. So the jealous brothers spread the word that Cinderlad could easily get it if he wanted to. And when the word reached the King, he called Cinderlad before him.

"I have heard that you can get me the Troll's bedspread," said the King.

"Oh dear," sighed the lad. "Who would say such a thing?"

"Your brothers," replied the King. "Your brothers said it would be easy for you to do."

"Then it must be true," said the lad. "I will do it, but I must wait until the day when the sun is shining at its brightest."

When that day arrived, the Troll brought his bedspread of spun silver and gold into a clearing in front of his cave. And he sat down to watch it sparkle in the sun.

Cinderlad quietly rowed across the lake and hid in the bushes. When the ugly old Troll went inside for a moment, the lad snatched the bedspread and began to row back across the lake. When he was halfway across, he heard the Troll stomping and puffing on the shore.

"Who dares to steal my bedspread of spun silver and gold?" roared the Troll.

"It is I," called Cinderlad, "the King's kitchen helper."

"Come back here!" roared the Troll.

"Perhaps I shall," replied the lad. "Perhaps I shall." But he kept on rowing until he was back at the King's palace.

When the King saw the bedspread of spun silver and gold, he was overjoyed. He praised

Cinderlad for his cunning and bravery, but the two brothers only grew more jealous. And they tried to think of some way to make trouble for their youngest brother.

It so happened that the ugly old Troll had a magic harp that was made of pure gold. Whenever the harp was played, all who listened became happy—no matter how sad they had been before. The King often wished he owned the harp. So the two jealous brothers spread the word that the kitchen helper could get it for him. When the King heard this, he sent for the youngest brother.

"I understand that you can get me the Troll's magic harp," said the King.

"Oh dear," sighed the lad. "Who would say such a thing?"

"Your brothers," replied the King. "Your brothers said it would be easy for you to do."

"Then it must be true," said Cinderlad. "I will do it."

"If you succeed," promised the King, "I will give you half my kingdom, and the hand of my daughter in marriage."

"Very well," said the lad. "But first, I will need a long iron nail, a wooden stick, and a thick candle."

When Cinderlad had the nail, the stick, and the candle, he rowed to the other side of the lake. The ugly old Troll came running out, stomping and puffing.

"Aha!" roared the Troll. "The King's kitchen helper!"

"Good morning," said Cinderlad.

"Don't 'good morning' me!" roared the Troll. "You stole my seven silver ducks!"

"So I did," replied Cinderlad.

"You stole my bedspread of spun silver and gold!" roared the Troll.

"So I did," replied the lad.

"Then you shall pay!" roared the Troll. He grabbed Cinderlad, and dragged him into his cave. A young Troll was stirring a bubbling pot over the fire.

"Fatten him up!" roared the ugly old Troll. "And when he is ready, put him into the pot!"

So the young Troll locked Cinderlad in the fattening cage, and fed him very rich foods. When a week had passed, the young Troll said, "Stick out your finger!" But the clever Cinderlad stuck out the long iron nail instead. The young Troll bit down on it and cried, "He's still as tough as nails!"

"Then feed him twice as much!" roared the ugly old Troll.

When another week had passed, the young Troll said, "Stick out your finger!" But Cinderlad stuck out the wooden stick instead. The young Troll bit down on it, and cried, "He's still as tough as the branch of a tree!"

"Then feed him three times as much!" roared the ugly old Troll.

When another week had passed, the young Troll said, "Stick out your finger!" This time, Cinderlad stuck out the thick candle. And this time, the young Troll bit down and cried, "Now he's ready for the pot!"

"Then we will feast on him tomorrow!" roared the ugly old Troll. "I will invite all the other Trolls to the feast."

The next morning, the young Troll got up before daybreak. He wanted to get Cinderlad into the pot early enough to cook him through and through. He took out a rusty old knife, and then he opened the fattening cage.

"Oh dear," said Cinderlad. "It would take you all day to cut me up with that old knife. Here, let me sharpen it for you." And he took the knife, and began to sharpen it. But as he worked, he looked past the young Troll—toward the door of the cave. It was still dark outside.

"That must be sharp enough," said the young Troll.

"No it isn't," said Cinderlad. He was waiting for the sun to rise. He kept on sharpening the knife.

"That's sharp enough now," cried the young Troll.

"Perhaps it is," replied Cinderlad, for at that very moment, he saw the first rays of the sun. "But the only way to test it is to split one of the hairs that grows on the back of a young Troll's head. Turn around, so I can get such a hair."

The young Troll turned around. And as he did, he was instantly turned into a cracked and aging stone. For that is what happens when a Troll is foolish enough to turn around and look into the rising sun.

Then Cinderlad dressed up as a young Troll, and began to stir the pot on the fire. Before long, the ugly old Troll awoke. Shortly after that, all the other Trolls arrived. They began to stomp and puff and dance about the cave. But the young Troll—who was really Cinderlad—sat in a corner and looked very sad.

"This is no time for sadness," roared the ugly old Troll. "Take out the magic harp and play it!"

"I don't remember where it is," replied Cinderlad.

"It is in its usual place!" roared the ugly old Troll. "Under the pile of bones in the corner!"

Cinderlad took out the harp and strolled back and forth among the guests, playing one tune after another. Before long, he had wandered out of the cave and down to the edge of the lake. Suddenly, he stopped playing the harp and jumped into his boat.

At once, the ugly old Troll came stomping and puffing out of the cave. "Who dares to steal my magic harp?" he roared.

"It is I—the King's kitchen helper," called Cinderlad, who was now rowing out across the lake.

"Then you are not in the pot?" roared the Troll, more angry than he had ever been before.

"Indeed I am not," called the lad.

The ugly old Troll was so upset that he stomped and he puffed and he blew himself up until he burst!

Cinderlad gave the magic harp to the King. Then he married the King's daughter and received half the kingdom.

And even though he was now very rich, he was kind to his brothers. After all, if they had not said what they said, he might still be the King's kitchen helper!

The Prince With the
Very Long Nose

Once there was a King who loved a Princess. But he could not marry her because she had been put under a spell by a wicked Troll. The Princess just sat all day long and stared out the window. Once in a while she would stroke the back of her large tabby cat. But that's all she ever did because of the enchantment.

Now the King happened to know a friendly Troll who was also very wise.

"There is only one way to break the spell," said the friendly Troll. "You must step on the tail of the tabby cat."

The King thought that sounded easy enough. So he quickly marched off to the castle where the Princess sat all day. There she was as usual, staring out the window. By her side sat her large, contented-looking tabby cat.

The King walked right up to the cat and quickly put his foot down. But the cat flicked its tail at just the right moment. The King's foot came down upon the floor. Time and again he tried, but the King could not step on the cat's tail.

"I think this cat might be enchanted too," said

the King. For seven days and seven nights, he tried to step on the cat's tail. But it was no use, for the cat always moved its tail—just in time.

Then, early one morning, the King was lucky enough to come upon the cat when it was taking a short nap. Quick as a wink, the King brought his foot down on the cat's tail.

At once, the cat turned into the wicked Troll who had cast the spell on the Princess.

"You have broken the enchantment," said the Troll. "But I shall have my revenge. You can marry the Princess, and make her your Queen. But before a year passes, you will die, and she will have a son. He will never be happy until he says 'my nose is too long.' And if you tell anyone what I have just said, you will die all the sooner."

The King laughed at the wicked Troll. But just to be on the safe side, he never told anyone what the Troll had said.

Very soon, the King married the Princess and made her his Queen. The King died within a year—just after his son was born. The baby had laughing eyes and curly hair. He also had a very, very long nose. Of course the Queen thought the boy's nose was beautiful. After all, he was her first child, and she loved every bit of him.

No one at the court was brave enough to tell

the Queen that her son had a very strange nose. No one dared to suggest that his nose was too long.

As the years passed and the Prince grew older, no one found the courage to tell him the truth about his nose. In fact, everyone took great care to convince him that his nose was perfect. All the lords and ladies of the court took to pulling on the noses of their children to make them more like the Prince's. As a result, some of the children did grow up with noses a little longer than usual. But no one had such a long nose as the Prince.

When he went to school, his teachers told him that all the great heroes had long noses. So the Prince never dreamed that his nose might be unusual. In fact, he wouldn't have parted with it for the world.

When the Prince reached his twentieth birthday, he fell in love with the Princess from the next kingdom. She was lovely indeed, although she did have a rather short nose.

One night, a great ball was held in honor of the Prince and the Princess. Suddenly, the wicked Troll appeared. He waved his hand, and a cloud of dust surrounded the Princess. And when the dust had settled, the Princess had disappeared.

The young Prince could not be comforted. In

great despair, he mounted his horse and set out to find his beloved.

He searched for many days, and finally came to a cave. Sitting inside the cave was a friendly Troll who was at least one-hundred years old.

When the Prince entered the cave, the Troll put on his eyeglasses to see him better. It took some time to adjust them, because the Troll's nose was very, very short, and his glasses kept falling off.

When the old Troll and the young Prince looked at each other closely, they both burst into laughter. "What a funny nose you have!" they both shouted.

The Prince was a little insulted. "Just what is the matter with my nose?" he demanded.

"Why, nothing is the *matter* with it, exactly," said the Troll. "Except that there is so *much* of it!" And the old Troll again burst into laughter.

"What a rude creature," thought the Prince. But he said nothing more.

"Make yourself at home," said the old Troll. "I know who you are. I was a very good friend of your dear father, the King. He often came to see me, and I advised him on many matters."

"Then perhaps you can help me, too," said the

Prince. "But first I would ask for some supper. I have traveled far, and I am very hungry."

"Certainly, I'll get you some food," said the Troll, "but let me tell you of a conversation I once had with your dear father. You don't remember him, I know, but his nose was fine, I assure you—just the right size—and not at all like yours." And the old Troll talked and talked, never stopping long enough to take a full breath.

"This old Troll certainly does talk a good deal," thought the Prince. "And I do wish he would stop all this talk about noses." Then, he said out loud, "I would gladly listen to any of your stories, but I'm sure I could listen better on a full stomach."

"Oh, of course," said the Troll. "I quite forgot you were hungry." The Troll called for his servants to bring some food for the Prince. And all the time the Troll kept talking and talking, hardly taking a breath, and chattering on and on about the Prince's father and the Prince's long, funny-looking nose.

As he ate, the Prince could see that the servants were secretly laughing at the Troll and his constant chatter.

"I am really glad I have met this old Troll," the Prince said to himself. "I see how his servants laugh at him. He does not realize how very much he talks. I am glad that *I* know how people really feel about me. I would never be taken in by those who act one way to my face and another way when I can't see them. At least I know my own faults!"

After supper, the old Troll was still talking, and the Prince never got the chance to ask the Troll's advice about rescuing the Princess.

So the Prince rode off, and continued looking for the Princess. Soon, he found himself in a very strange land. Everyone he met seemed to stare at his nose. "I don't understand this," said the Prince. "There must be something wrong with all these people."

Meanwhile, the friendly old Troll had been busy. He knew that the Prince was searching for the Princess. So with his magic powers, he located the place where the wicked Troll had hidden her. Then he whisked the Princess from her hiding place and put her in a glass palace. He set the palace down in the middle of a great clearing, where the Prince would be sure to find her.

Sure enough, before long the Prince rode up to the glass palace. And there inside was his beautiful Princess. Oh, how happy they were to see each other! The Prince tried to break the walls of

the palace to free the Princess. He tried smashing the walls with his sword. He tried hitting the walls with rocks. But the walls would not break.

Finally, the Prince found one tiny opening in one wall. It was just big enough for the Princess to put her hand through. The Prince took her hand and bent to kiss it. But try as he might, he could not touch her hand with his lips. His nose was always in the way.

After many tries, the Prince said, "How distressing. I cannot seem to get close enough, for my nose is too long."

And in that instant, the glass palace shattered into a million pieces. The Prince and the Princess rushed into each other's arms.

Suddenly, the friendly old Troll appeared before them. "You have broken the enchantment because you have admitted the truth," he said. "Sometimes we are too vain to see the truth about ourselves."

The Prince knew that what the old Troll said was true. And he never forgot the lesson. The Prince's nose remained as it was—very long. But that didn't matter. For he was a kind and good Prince, no matter how long his nose was.

The Prince and the Princess were married in

great splendor. The wedding feast went on for three full days, and the Prince and the Princess lived happily for the rest of their lives.